Franklin's New Friend

ISBN 0-590-02592-9

Text copyright © 1997 by Paulette Bourgeois
Illustrations copyright © 1997 by Brenda Clark
FRANKLIN and the FRANKLIN character are trademarks of Kids Can Press Ltd.
All rights reserved. Published by Scholastic Inc., 555 Broadway, New York, NY 10012, by arrangement with Kids Can Press Ltd.
Interior illustrations prepared with the assistance of Muriel Hughes Wood.

12 11 10 9 8 7 6 5 4 3 2 1   7 8 9/9 0 1 2/0

Printed in the U.S.A.   23

First Scholastic printing, September 1997

Franklin's New Friend

Paulette Bourgeois
Brenda Clark

SCHOLASTIC INC.

New York   Toronto   London   Auckland   Sydney

FRANKLIN had always lived in the same house in the same town. He had grown up with his friends, and each one had a special place in Franklin's life.

When Franklin wanted to play hide and seek, he called Fox. If Franklin needed a best friend, he called Bear.

Franklin never thought about making friends until a new family moved in down the lane.

Franklin was curious about the newcomers.
He rubbed his eyes as the movers unloaded
the furniture. The beds were made for giants,
and the lamps were as tall as trees.
    When Franklin finally saw the family, he
was speechless.

Franklin had never met a moose before. He had heard about moose. He had seen pictures of moose. But he had never actually known one. They were huge. Even the smallest moose was big.

Franklin was so scared that he raced home.

"A moose family moved in!"

"That's nice," said Franklin's mother. "Maybe you'll make a new friend."

Franklin shook his head. "I don't think so."

"I expect you to be nice when you meet someone new," warned his mother.

Franklin scowled.

The next morning, there was a moose in Franklin's classroom.

"Please give a warm welcome to your new classmate," said Mr. Owl.

"Hello, Moose," said the class in unison.
Moose mumbled hello and looked at his feet.
"He doesn't look very friendly," whispered Beaver.

Mr. Owl told the class that Moose had come from a different place, far away.

"Franklin," said Mr. Owl, "I'd like you to be a buddy for Moose."

Franklin tried to smile but he was scared. Moose was so big!

Moose didn't say a word all morning.

At recess, Franklin ran outside with his friends, leaving Moose behind. But Mr. Owl reminded Franklin that he was Moose's buddy.

"Do you want to play?" asked Franklin.

Moose shook his head back and forth.

Franklin was relieved.

During recess, Moose stood alone as Franklin
and his friends played soccer.

Fox kicked the ball too hard, and it flew into
a tree.

"Now we'll have to get Mr. Owl," groaned Bear.

"I've got it!" cried Moose. He knocked the ball
out of the tree and sent it flying to Franklin.

"That was good," said Fox.

"I guess," shrugged Franklin.

Back in the classroom, Mr. Owl asked Franklin and Moose to make a poster for the bake sale.

"I don't need any help," said Franklin.

Mr. Owl talked to Franklin alone. "Try to imagine how Moose feels. He's new and he has no friends here. He's probably scared."

"Moose can't be scared," said Franklin. "He's so big."

Mr. Owl looked at Franklin. "Big or little, we all get scared."

Franklin thought about that.

Franklin got the paints and the paper.
"Do you want to help me, Moose?"
"Oh, yes," said Moose. "I love to draw."
They sat side by side and planned the
poster together.
Franklin realized that Moose didn't seem
as big when he was sitting.

After much work, the poster was perfect. They both thought so.

At library time, Franklin taught Moose how to borrow books.

Moose showed Franklin how to cut a
perfect circle.
They both liked to build structures.
Franklin and Moose had a lot in common.

At lunch, Franklin made sure that Bear and his other friends got to know his new buddy.

They liked Moose. Besides, he was a very good soccer player.

When Franklin got home from school, he was happy.

"Guess what?" he told his mother. "I have a new friend."

"So you met Moose?" asked his mother. "What's he like?"

"Moose is big," said Franklin. "But he's not mean or scary."

"Good," said his mother. "Would you like to take some of these cookies to him?"

Franklin went to Moose's house.
They ate all the cookies together.
"I'm glad you were my buddy," said
Moose. "I was worried that nobody would
play with me."
"Really?" said Franklin. He could barely
remember being afraid of Moose.

From then on, Franklin and Moose
played together all the time. Now Franklin's
new friend was a special friend.